Magic Puppy

To Pash—gorgeous, charming spotty girl . . .
except for the snail-crunching!—SB

GROSSET & DUNLAP
Published by the Penguin Group
Penguin Group (USA) Inc., 375 Hudson Street, New York, New York 10014, USA

USA | Canada | UK | Ireland | Australia | New Zealand | India | South Africa | China
Penguin Books Ltd, Registered Offices: 80 Strand, London WC2R 0RL, England

For more information about the Penguin Group visit penguin.com

Text copyright © 2009 Sue Bentley. Illustrations copyright © 2009 Angela Swan.
Cover illustration © 2009 Andrew Farley. First printed in Great Britain in 2009
by Penguin Books Ltd. First published in the United States in 2013 by Grosset & Dunlap,
a division of Penguin Young Readers Group, 345 Hudson Street, New York, New York 10014.
GROSSET & DUNLAP is a trademark of Penguin Group (USA) Inc. Printed in the U.S.A.

Library of Congress Cataloging-in-Publication Data is available.

ISBN 978-0-448-46732-0   10 9 8 7 6 5 4 3 2

Magic Puppy

Classroom Princess

SUE BENTLEY

Illustrated by Angela Swan

Grosset & Dunlap
An Imprint of Penguin Group (USA) Inc.

Prologue

Storm glanced up at the snow clouds gathering over the dark mountaintops. It felt good to be back in his home world.

Suddenly, the young silver-gray wolf stiffened as a terrifying howl echoed through the still air. "Shadow!" Storm gasped. The fierce lone wolf who had attacked the Moon-claw pack was very close.

He should have known that it was not safe to return. He needed to find a place to hide, and quickly.

There was a dazzling flash of bright light and a shower of gold sparks. Where the young wolf had been standing, there now crouched a tiny, fluffy brown-and-white King Charles spaniel puppy with bright midnight-blue eyes and a silky tail.

Storm hoped this disguise would protect him until he found a place to hide.

The tiny puppy's heart beat fast as he leaped forward and bounded up a steep hill. Storm looked from right to left as he ran, his floppy little ears flying out behind him, but there was nowhere to hide. No scrubby trees or bushes, not even a clump of grass.

Storm felt himself growing tired. Then he spotted a cluster of rocks. Perhaps there would be a small space he could squeeze into. But suddenly the dark shape of a large wolf came into view. The tiny puppy whimpered with alarm.

This was it. Shadow had found him!

"This way, my son!" called the wolf in a deep, velvety growl. "There is a cave where we will be safe for a while."

"Mother!" Storm woofed in relief. He scrambled over the rocks and followed Canista as she led him down into the cave.

As the darkness closed over Storm, he licked his mother's muzzle in greeting, wriggling his whole body and wagging his tail.

Canista reached out a huge gray paw that was bigger than Storm was now and pulled her disguised cub against her warm, furry side.

"I am glad to see you again, but you have returned at a dangerous time. Shadow is hunting for you. He wants to lead the Moon-claw pack, but the others will not follow him. They will wait until you are strong enough to become the leader."

Storm's bright blue eyes flared with anger and sorrow. "Is it not enough that Shadow has killed my father and all my brothers and wounded you? Let us fight him and force him to leave our land!"

Canista's face softened as she gazed at her brave little pup. "I am still too weak from Shadow's poisonous bite, and you cannot face him alone. Use this disguise. Go back to the other world and return when you are stronger."

As she finished speaking, Storm saw

her face cloud with pain. He leaned forward and huffed out a warm puppy breath filled with a thousand tiny gold stars. The sparkling mist swirled around Canista's sore leg for a moment before it sank into her fur and disappeared.

"Thank you. The pain is lessening," she growled softly.

Suddenly, there came the sound of mighty paws digging at the rocks outside. An enormous wolf's head was outlined against the sky at the cave's entrance.

"Go, Storm! Save yourself!" Canista urged. Storm whimpered as bright gold sparks ignited in his fluffy brown-and-white fur and he felt the power building inside him. A bright golden glow grew around him. And it grew brighter still . . .

Chapter
ONE

Kelsey Fisher frowned as she saw a car pull up outside. The doors sprang open, and her dad's new girlfriend, Jo Wright, and her twin daughters got out.

What are they *doing here so early?* Kelsey wondered.

It was Saturday morning, and she was still in her pajamas. They had been a Christmas present from her mom, who

now lived in Australia with her new
husband and Kelsey's younger half brother.
The pajamas had a pattern of little blue
teddy bears with pink bows, and Kelsey
adored them—even though they were
getting to be a little too small for her.

As footsteps came thundering up the
stairs, Kelsey quickly leaped back into bed
and dived under the covers to hide her
pajamas from the older girls.

The bedroom door banged open, and Anna and Louise burst into her room.

"Surprise!" Anna said cheerfully. "Mom's taking us all to the new riding stables."

"You're coming, too! There's probably a nice, quiet pony you can ride," Louise added.

Kelsey couldn't think of anything worse. Ponies terrified her. There was no way she was going anywhere near one—nice and quiet, or not. But if the twins found out that she was scared of ponies, they'd tease her even more than they usually did.

"Thanks . . . but I'm . . . er . . . not really feeling great," she said quickly.

"That's what you think!" Anna grabbed Kelsey's pillow and started bashing her with it. *Whump! Whump!*

"Give that back!" Kelsey cried, leaping up and making a lunge for her pillow.

"What funny pj's. They don't even fit you!" Louise said, giggling.

Kelsey blushed hotly. She tried to pull the pillow away from Anna, but Anna was bigger than she was and much stronger. Anna threw the pillow to Louise, who caught it and tossed it on to the floor and then both of them pulled the covers off Kelsey's bed.

"Now you *have* to get up!" Anna crowed.

Kelsey's dad appeared in the bedroom doorway. "What's all this noise about? Ah, a pillow fight! Having fun?" he said, smiling.

It's not fun, when it's one-sided, Kelsey

thought bitterly. *Or should that be two-sided, if it involves twins?*

"We're trying to persuade Kelsey to come out with us. But she doesn't want to," Louise cried.

Her dad frowned. "Why's that, Kelsey?"

Kelsey scrunched herself up against the back of her bed and folded her arms tightly across her chest. "I can't go, because . . . I've got . . . um . . . tummy ache. I must have eaten too much pizza last night," she said.

Jo peered over Kelsey's dad's shoulder. "Why's everyone in here?" she asked, puzzled. Jo had a friendly smile and gentle blue eyes.

"Kelsey's not coming with us, Mom. She overdid it with the pizza!" Anna said.

"Poor old you." Jo's pretty face creased in concern as she looked at Kelsey. "Would you like to just come and watch? You might feel better in the fresh air."

Kelsey stared at the floor. "I'd rather just stay here with Dad," she said quietly.

"Maybe that would be best. It's a shame you're sick, but you can always come riding another time," Jo said kindly.

"Come on, you two. We'd better get going. I hope you feel better soon, Kelsey. See you later."

The twins followed their mom out. "See ya! Wouldn't wanna be ya!" they chorused from the doorway.

Kelsey tingled with embarrassment as she heard them giggling all the way down the stairs. Her dad went down to the front door to see them out and the house was suddenly quiet.

Kelsey sighed. She wasn't sure how she felt about her dad having a girlfriend. It had been fine for the last couple of years with just the two of them. Jo seemed nice, and Kelsey thought she might even get to like her, but the twins were so hyper and full of themselves. Kelsey didn't even know if she wanted to be friends with them.

Mr. Fisher came back into the room as Kelsey was making her bed.

"Those twins are real firecrackers, aren't they? You'll have to start sticking up for yourself a bit more around them, honey," he commented.

Kelsey nodded, blinking hard so he wouldn't notice her tears. That was easy for *him* to say. "Will you be okay by

yourself for a while, if I start doing some work?" he asked, ruffling her curly light-brown hair. Her dad designed and built websites and sometimes worked from home.

Kelsey managed a shaky smile. "I've stopped feeling so sick now. I think I'll go and read in the old summer house to cheer myself up."

"Good idea. You love it down there. Don't forget to bundle up. It feels mild today, but it's still only January."

"I will," she told him. "You're right. Give me a shout if you need anything." As soon as he left, Kelsey leaped out of bed and threw on her clothes. Grabbing her favorite book of dog stories and a fleece blanket, she went outside and down to the bottom of the garden. The summer house was a small wooden building nestling among the trees. She had played there with her dolls when she was little, and a lot of her old toys were still stored there.

Kelsey found a cozy chair and snuggled up inside her blanket to read. The stories were so thrilling that she didn't notice the time passing. One hour and then another ticked by. She was in the middle of a really exciting story about a lost puppy when, suddenly, a dazzling flash of bright gold light lit up the entire summer house.

"Oh!" Kelsey almost jumped out of her skin. It must have been lightning. She looked up from her book, expecting to hear a roll of thunder at any moment.

To her amazement, right in front of her was a tiny, fluffy brown-and-white

puppy. It looked up at her with enormous
midnight-blue eyes. "Please help me," it
woofed.

Chapter
TWO

Kelsey did a double take. The book slipped off her lap and landed on the floor with a *thud*. She must have been so engrossed in her story that she'd just imagined the tiny puppy had spoken to her!

There was a big fence all around the garden, and Kelsey couldn't figure out how the tiny puppy could have climbed over it. Shrugging off the blanket, she got

out of the chair and looked down at the
tiny puppy in front of her. "Hello there.
Where did you come from?"

The puppy put its head on one side.
"I used my magic to come to this world. I
need to hide from my enemies. My name
is Storm of the Moon-claw pack. What is
yours?" it woofed politely.

"Oh!" Kelsey gasped, taking a step
back. As the backs of her knees bumped
into her chair, she sat down again with a
jolt. "You . . . you really can . . . sp-speak!"
she stammered.

The puppy nodded. He sat down
and curled his silky tail around his little
brown-and-white body. Despite his tiny
size, Storm didn't seem to be afraid of
Kelsey. He was looking at her curiously
and seemed to be waiting for her to reply.

"I'm . . . um . . . Kelsey. Kelsey Fisher," she said. "I live here in Long Morton with my dad."

Storm dipped his tiny head in a formal bow. "I am honored to meet you, Kelsey."

"Um . . . me too," Kelsey said.

She was still having trouble taking all this in, but she didn't want to frighten this amazing little puppy away. Kelsey slowly got up again and then crouched down to make herself seem smaller and less threatening.

"Why do you need to hide? Is someone after you?" she asked softly.

Storm's blue eyes darkened as he nodded. "A fierce lone wolf attacked my Moon-claw pack. He is called Shadow. Shadow killed my father and brothers and wounded my mother. He wants to be leader, but the other wolves want to wait until I can lead them."

Kelsey blinked at him in surprise. "But how can you lead a wolf pack? You're just a tiny pup—"

"Keep back, please!" Storm ordered. Before Kelsey knew what was happening, there was another brilliant flash of light and a fountain of gold sparks gushed out all around her, before drifting harmlessly to the summer-house floor.

The tiny brown-and-white puppy had disappeared and in its place a regal-looking young silver-gray wolf stood there proudly, almost filling the summer house. Its thick neck ruff glimmered with thousands of tiny lights that shined like gems.

"Storm?" Kelsey asked anxiously,

eyeing the young wolf's sharp teeth,
enormous paws, and muscular body.

"Yes, Kelsey, it is me. Do not be afraid.
I will not harm you," Storm said in a deep,
velvety growl.

Before Kelsey had time to get used to
Storm in this majestic form, there was a
final, dazzling bright flash of gold light and
he reappeared as a tiny, fluffy brown-and-
white puppy with huge midnight-blue
eyes.

"Oh! That was incredible!" Kelsey

breathed. "What a brilliant disguise."

"Yes, but Shadow will see through it, if he finds me," Storm yapped softly. "I am in danger. I need to hide now."

Kelsey saw that the tiny puppy had tucked his tail between his back legs and was beginning to tremble all over. Her heart went out to him. Storm was stunning as his real wolf self, but as a small ball of soft brown–and–white fur he was totally adorable.

Kelsey held out her hand and rubbed the tips of her fingers together encouragingly. Storm edged closer until his little, wet brown nose brushed her fingers. Kelsey picked him up, and Storm licked her chin with his pink tongue.

Smiling, Kelsey stroked his soft little head. "What am I going to do with you?

You'll be lonely hiding in the summer house all by yourself. I'll ask Dad if I can keep you. He'll understand. He knows that I've always wanted a puppy to be my special friend and sleep in my bedroom."

Storm showed his sharp little teeth in a doggy grin. "I would like that very much."

"Let's go into the office and ask him now. I can't wait to tell Dad all about you—" Kelsey broke off as Storm reared up and placed one tiny brown-and-white front paw on her cheek.

"No! You can tell no one my secret. You must promise me, Kelsey," he yapped, his little heart-shaped face suddenly serious.

Kelsey felt disappointed that she couldn't share her exciting news with her dad. He would have loved to know about Storm. But it would have to be a really special secret all of her own—one that not even the twins would know about.

"Okay. I promise. Cross my heart. No one's going to hear about you from me," she said.

Storm's muzzle lifted with a grin.

"Thank you, Kelsey."

As Kelsey stepped out of the summer house with Storm in her arms, she saw Anna and Louise striding down the lawn toward her. They looked hot and red-faced, and their boots and jeans were muddy.

"You just missed a brilliant riding lesson—" Anna began and then her eyes widened as she spotted Storm. "Wow! Where did that cute puppy come from?"

"Did your dad buy it for us all to share? Give it to me. I want to hold it!" Louise ordered, holding out her arms.

Kelsey stood there uncertainly, feeling tongue-tied by her usual shyness. But then a surge of protectiveness for Storm swept over her. "Storm's a *he*, not an *it*," she found herself blurting, to her own surprise. "I'd better hold him for now. He's very nervous until he gets used to people."

Louise and Anna exchanged amazed glances. Kelsey marched past them while they were silent for once.

Chapter
THREE

"I don't know, Kelsey, you know how I feel about kids having pets," Mr. Fisher said ten minutes later when Kelsey had finished giving her version of how she had found Storm in the summer house. "They have a habit of getting bored with them in no time, and then the poor old parents are the ones who have to look after them. I think we'll phone the local shelter. I'm sure they will find him a good home."

Kelsey and Storm stood in the small kitchen, next to Jo and the twins. "But I won't get bored with Storm! He's special, Dad! He chose me to look after him," Kelsey exclaimed. *Oh no, she hadn't meant to say that! She must be more careful.*

Luckily her dad just laughed. "You and your imagination, Kelsey Fisher!"

Kelsey bit her lip, feeling her face flush. How could she change her dad's mind? He just *had* to let Storm live with them. Storm was in danger, and only she could keep him safe.

"Please, Dad," she rushed on. "I promise that I'll look after him. He can sleep in my room, and I'll buy his food from my allowance and everything."

Mr. Fisher looked surprised. "Well,

I haven't seen you this passionate about something for a while! You're usually such a quiet little mouse. Is this really important to you?"

"D-Definitely." Kelsey gulped.

"Storm looks like a little King Charles spaniel," Jo commented. She turned to Kelsey's dad. "Maybe it would be a good idea for Kelsey to look after him, at least

until his owner turns up. Being responsible for a pet can do a lot for a person's self-confidence," she said.

Mr. Fisher wavered. "That's true," he said, looking at Kelsey thoughtfully.

Kelsey didn't even mind that they were talking about her as if she wasn't standing right there. "So, can I keep him then, Dad?" she asked, crossing her fingers and all her toes. "Storm can sleep in my bedroom and—"

"That's not fair! Storm should live at our house sometimes if we're going to share him," Louise grumbled.

"Yeah. He's going to be our dog, too, isn't he? I'm going to get him a collar and a chew toy from the pet store," Anna cried.

"But he's not your . . ." Kelsey's

shoulders sagged and her voice trailed off. The twins were impossible when they were in full-on bossy mode. She wished she could just point the TV remote at them and press the PAUSE button.

Jo stepped forward. "Hold your horses, you two!" she snapped at the twins. "Who said anything about puppy-sharing? Storm belongs to Kelsey. She found him in her summer house, so he's her responsibility. I'm sure she'll ask us for help if she needs it. Isn't that right, Kelsey?"

Kelsey nodded.

"Aw, Mom!" the twins complained.

"That's enough! I'm not going to argue with you," Jo said in a warning tone.

The twins got the message.

Kelsey was too amazed to speak. She had never expected Jo to be on *her* side.

Her dad smiled in his usual easygoing way. "Well, it looks as if that's settled. You can keep Storm, Kelsey. But if his owner turns up, there'll be no arguments. Understood?"

Kelsey nodded happily. She knew that no one was going to come and claim this particular puppy! "Thanks, Dad. I'm just

going to take Storm upstairs to make him
a bed, and then I'll go to the store to buy
him some food." She beamed gratefully at
Jo on her way out. "Um . . . thanks," she
said quietly.

Jo smiled back, her blue eyes twinkling.
She squeezed Kelsey's shoulder gently.
"You're welcome!"

Halfway up the stairs, Kelsey paused
with Storm in her arms, half expecting
Anna and Louise to come racing after
her and insist on "helping" her with the
puppy. But no one followed her. It actually
seemed quiet and calm downstairs.

When she got to her room, Kelsey
kissed the top of Storm's fluffy little head
and then placed him on her bed, where
he turned in circles before making himself
comfortable.

"I like it here. This is a safe place," Storm said with a yawn.

Kelsey smiled at him. She felt a warm glow of happiness as she realized that she now had a special, magical friend—and a secret just for herself.

"Are you going to be okay while I'm at school today?" Kelsey asked Storm after breakfast on Monday morning.

Storm was curled up on her lap under the table. "I will come with you. I like school," he woofed.

Kelsey looked down at him in amazement. Storm knew about school? He was full of surprises.

"Well, okay, then," she said, still not quite sure about having a puppy in

her class all day. "But I'll have to hide
you inside my school bag, in case Miss
Armitage notices you. She's my teacher."

Storm's big midnight-blue eyes looked
at her with eagerness. "Do not worry. I
will use my magic so that only you can
see and hear me."

"You can make yourself invisible? Cool! There's no problem, then!" Kelsey said delightedly. "Maybe you should do it now in case Dad sees you leaving with me."

Kelsey felt a slight tingling sensation down her spine. Little gold sparks bloomed in Storm's silky brown-and-white fur and then faded immediately.

"It is done," Storm woofed.

C h a p t e r
FOUR

Kelsey walked to school with Storm trotting along invisibly beside her. She still expected someone to notice her new puppy and ask about him. When no one did, she slowly began to relax, smiling at the thought of her very special secret.

As Kelsey and Storm walked through the school gates, Kelsey spotted Anna and Louise. The twins were one grade above

her and were standing and chatting with a
group of older girls.

"Hiya, Kelsey," Anna shouted, waving
eagerly.

"Hey! How's that mega gorgeous little
puppy?" boomed Louise.

Kelsey hid a smile as she thought how amazed they would be if they knew that Storm was right under their noses, but of course they couldn't see him! "Storm's fine, thanks," she answered.

"We're coming over to your house with Mom after school tomorrow. And Louise and me are going to take Storm for a walk just to help you out," Anna said enthusiastically.

"That's okay. I'm doing fine with him, thanks," Kelsey said, determined not to let the twins take up all of Storm's time. Anna didn't reply, and Kelsey was surprised to see that she actually looked crestfallen.

"Haven't you ever heard that sharing is caring?" one of the girls from the twins' group called out. Kelsey's heart began thumping as the whole group of older girls all turned to look at her.

Kelsey ignored them, and luckily the next moment the bell rang and she turned quickly toward the safety of her classroom.

Surprised by Kelsey's sudden movement, Storm scampered forward, almost tripping her up. Kelsey did a hasty sidestep to avoid treading on the little puppy, and bumped straight into a boy from her class.

"Oof!" It was Ross Kirk, a new boy who had only lived in Long Morton for a few months. There was a *thud* as the pile of books Ross was carrying crashed to the ground.

The twins and their friends all giggled. Kelsey went hot. She hated how she blushed all the time.

"Watch out!" Ross said crossly, going

redder than Kelsey. Even his ears glowed.

"Sorry, Ross," Kelsey murmured. She bent down to pick up one of the books, but some loose pages fluttered out and were whipped across the playground by a stiff breeze. "I'll get them!" she called.

As Kelsey ran about chasing pages, Storm scampered around helpfully snapping pages out of the air and jumping on others, so that Kelsey could gather them all up.

"Thanks, Storm," Kelsey whispered as she returned with the book to Ross. "Um . . . sorry. Some of the pages got a bit messed up."

"I can see that!" Ross complained, looking confused at what Kelsey realized were puppy teeth marks! "This is a school library book. You know how Miss

Armitage is always going on about how we're supposed to look after them. I'll probably get double detention."

Kelsey felt really bad for him. She wanted to help, but didn't know what she could do.

But Storm did. He jumped up, pawing at her skirt to get her attention. "Ask Ross to give the book to you!" he woofed.

Kelsey wasn't sure what Storm was planning, but she already trusted him. She didn't hesitate. "Give me the book, Ross. I'll . . . um . . . try and fix it."

Ross frowned suspiciously, but he handed it over. "Okay, then. But if Miss Armitage asks me where it is, I'm telling her you've got it. I'm not doing detention for you as well as me!" Thrusting his hands into his pockets, he went into the school.

All the other kids had gone inside
now, including Anna, Louise, and their
friends. Kelsey stood in the empty
playground with Storm.

"Wow! Ross is moody, isn't he?
Anyone would think I dropped his book
on purpose," she said, looking down at

Storm. "Why did you want him to give it to me anyway?"

Storm's little muzzle creased in a mysterious smile, and Kelsey felt another warm, prickling sensation flow down her spine. But it was much stronger this time.

Glittering sparks glowed in Storm's brown-and-white fur and his little floppy ears crackled with electricity. Lifting a front paw, he sent a glittering jet of sparks whooshing toward the battered library book in Kelsey's hands.

She watched in complete amazement as the book fanned open by itself. A swarm of sparkles like tiny fireflies whizzed between the pages. They rubbed out muddy marks, smoothed out creases and teeth marks, and stuck all the loose pages back in place.

In no time at all, the book was as good as new. Then it closed with a loud *snap!* and Kelsey saw that every last golden spark had faded from Storm's silky fur.

"That's fantastic. It's as good as new. Thanks, Storm!"

"You are welcome," he woofed.

Kelsey grinned at him, wondering what else her marvelous little friend could do.

Storm sat on Kelsey's lap while Miss Armitage took attendance, but he soon jumped down and went exploring.

Kelsey smiled as she saw him snuffling around the school bag of one of her classmates. She thought that he could probably smell the girl's pet dog or cat.

"Now, class, pay attention," Miss Armitage said. She had lovely curly dark-red hair, which she wore in a ponytail. "As you know we've been looking at festivals, such as Diwali, Easter, and Rosh Hashanah this term. And this weekend we'll be celebrating our local Wassail Night festival here in Long Morton. Now, I've got some very exciting news for you. This year's Wassail Apple Prince and Princess will both be chosen from *this* class."

Some of the students started cheering and clapping.

"Yay! I hope it's me, Miss!" said Mandy, a girl with long dark hair and olive skin.

Kelsey hoped it would be Mandy, too. She didn't want to wear a crown and cloak and lead the procession through the old orchard in front of hundreds of people.

From the corner of her eye, Kelsey noticed Storm ambling back toward her. He jumped onto her lap and then climbed up onto her desk. As he sat down, his silky tail swept against her pencil case and she just caught it before it was knocked to the floor.

Kelsey gasped, but luckily everyone was listening to the teacher and no one noticed.

"I am sorry," Storm yapped.

"Doesn't matter. No one saw. Did you have a good sniff around?" Kelsey whispered, smiling.

Storm nodded. "Yes. There are lots of exciting smells in here," he panted happily, his pink tongue hanging out.

"Pay attention, please, Kelsey. Who can

tell me what *wassail* means?" Miss
Armitage's voice rang out.

"Good health," a boy called Simon cried.

"Simon's right. It's from the Anglo-
Saxon *wes hal*. Does anyone know how long
the wassail tradition goes back?" Miss
Armitage looked pointedly at Kelsey.

Kelsey pretended that she hadn't
noticed and slipped down in her seat.

"Kelsey, please sit up straight!" the
teacher said briskly. "Answer the question,
now. Speak up, dear."

"Um . . . does it go back hundreds of
years?" Kelsey guessed, willing herself not
to blush.

Miss Armitage nodded her approval.
"Kelsey's right. Although no one knows
for sure, Wassail was probably invented by
farmers who were tired and worn out after

the Christmas holiday. They knew they
had hard winter work to look forward to,
and they needed something to pick them
up."

"My grandma has a pick-me-up every
night in her cocoa," Simon said with a
smile.

Miss Armitage gave him one of her
looks. A lot of kids laughed.

Despite herself, Kelsey couldn't help
smiling. She noticed that Ross wasn't
laughing. He sat by himself, looking pale
and tense.

"Get your workbooks out, please.
You can start on your designs for musical
instruments and lanterns," Miss Armitage
said.

Kelsey began working on a drawing
for her lantern. While everyone was

occupied, the teacher scribbled down everyone's name on scraps of paper and put them into a small bag.

Kelsey looked up from her drawing for a moment and saw that Ross still wore the same tense expression. He hadn't drawn very much, either. "I wonder if he's still worried about getting into trouble because of his library book," she whispered to Storm.

She didn't think she could risk skipping over to Ross's desk with the book. Miss Armitage was bound to see and ask awkward questions. She'd have to give it to him later.

Storm craned his little neck to look at Ross. "He seems like a very quiet boy."

Kelsey nodded. "He doesn't speak to many people in class, and I don't think he's made many friends. He must be lonely."

Storm's furry little brow wrinkled in a frown.

Kelsey had just turned back to the lantern design when she suddenly felt a familiar warm, tingling sensation down her backbone. She gave a small gasp as bright gold sparks ignited in Storm's brown-and-white fur and his floppy little ears fizzed with magical power.

What was happening?

A big streak of golden glitter shot straight at Ross. It bounced off him at a sharp angle and whizzed toward Miss Armitage. Some of the glitter flowed into the small bag she was holding and then shot back toward Kelsey. The golden sparkles swirled around Kelsey for a few seconds and then disappeared, just like that, leaving her with a very suspicious feeling.

Chapter
FIVE

"Storm? What did you just do?" Kelsey asked in an urgent whisper. She looked around the classroom, but everything looked just as it always did.

"I have found a way to make sure that Ross makes lots of friends!" Storm woofed, looking pleased with himself.

"Well, that's really sweet," Kelsey said carefully. "But how are you going to do that?"

"You will see." Storm's eyes glinted mysteriously. Lifting a little back leg, he began cleaning his toes.

Kelsey blinked. Storm was obviously up to something. What could it be?

"Can everyone stop whatever they're doing? I'm about to draw the names," Miss Armitage called out. Once everyone had settled down, she shook the bag and then took out two slips of paper and unfolded them. "This year's Apple Prince and Princess will be . . ." she said, pausing for effect, "Ross Kirk and Kelsey Fisher!"

"Yay! Three cheers for Ross and Kelsey. Hip-hip . . ."

As everyone began cheering, Kelsey sat there in stunned silence. "Oh no," she whispered to Storm. "I can't do this!" She felt herself going hot and cold at the thought of having to lead the Wassail procession.

Ross was staring across at her with his mouth open. He looked as if he wished the floor would open up and swallow him.

Storm gave Kelsey an encouraging grin that showed his sharp little teeth. "But it is good. Everyone will want to talk to you and Ross. You can help him

not to feel so shy, and he will make many
friends!" he yapped.

Kelsey couldn't answer Storm with
the whole class looking at her. She didn't
get a chance to speak to him until recess.
"Storm!" she scolded, once they were
by themselves. "I don't want to be Apple
Princess. You'll have to use your magic
to make Miss Armitage choose someone
else!"

The tiny puppy's ears drooped. "I am
afraid I cannot do that. The decision has
already been announced."

Kelsey sighed deeply. "Oh, that's just great! Thanks for nothing!"

Storm tucked his tail between his legs. "You are angry with me. I will leave if you want me to," he whimpered.

"Oh no, please don't do that!" Kelsey burst out hurriedly. She had been so concerned about how she felt that she'd forgotten about Storm's feelings. She pretended to bend down and fiddle with her shoe so that she could stroke him.

"I'm sorry. I'm not really cross. I never want you to leave!" she declared. It was true, she thought. Storm hadn't been her friend for long, but she couldn't imagine life without him now.

Storm perked up again. Wagging his tail, he wriggled his body and licked her hand.

Kelsey smiled. "I'll just have to put up with being the Apple Princess, won't I? It might not be so bad if I have you with me." She fought down the sinking feeling in her tummy.

"I will help you!" Storm yapped eagerly.

"Thanks. But ask me first next time, okay?" Kelsey said.

Storm nodded and raised one front paw. "That means, I promise!"

Kelsey smiled at his little face. "Let's go and find Ross and give him his book back."

When Kelsey handed the book to Ross, he just gaped at her.

"It's all mended. How did . . . ?"

"I'm just naturally brilliant at fixing things!" she joked. *At least, Storm is,* she thought, imagining Ross's face if he knew the truth. "So no one's getting double detention!"

*

Kelsey and Storm had just turned onto her street after school the following day. She saw the car parked outside her house and remembered that Jo and the twins were coming around.

As she walked into the front garden, the house door opened, and Anna and Louise came bouncing out. "Hiya, Kelsey!" they chorused.

"Hi," Kelsey greeted them.

"Me and Louise were going to take Storm for a walk before you got back from school," Anna said.

"We looked everywhere for him, even

in your bedroom, but we can't find him,"
Louise put in. "Your dad thinks he might
have run away again."

Kelsey felt a stir of frustration. It didn't
seem to occur to the twins that she might
not like them poking around in her room.

"Storm's . . . er . . . got a secret hiding
place he goes to when I'm at school,"
Kelsey stammered. "You two stay here. I'll
go and find him."

She went upstairs and changed out of
her school clothes and then came back
down to the sitting room with Storm
trotting beside her.

"There he is!" shrieked Louise,
kneeling down and making a big fuss over
Storm.

"Where were you hiding, you naughty
boy?" Anna scolded. She rolled Storm onto

his back and tickled his pale tummy.

Storm gave a small yelp of surprise.
"Be careful with him. He's very tiny,"
Kelsey said sharply.

The twins looked at her in surprise.
"Sorry, Storm," Anna said in a subdued
voice, being more gentle.

"You did not need to worry, Kelsey.

Anna and Louise were not hurting me," Storm woofed, when the twins moved away.

Kelsey nodded. "I know that, really. I didn't mean to snap. It's just that I can't get used to having the twins around here all the time. I liked it when it was just Dad and me," she whispered.

Her dad came into the room. He'd just ordered a pizza for dinner. "It'll be at least half an hour. They're really busy," he said.

"There's just time for Louise and me to take Storm for a walk, then. Can we, Kelsey?" Anna asked.

Kelsey sighed to herself. Once the twins got an idea in their heads, they never let up. She still didn't like the idea of letting Storm out of her sight. But what excuse could she give now for refusing to let anyone else take him for a walk?

Jo came in and put some more
logs into the wood-burning stove.
"Congratulations, by the way!" she said
to Kelsey, with a broad grin. "It's quite an
honor to be the Apple Princess and lead
the procession."

"Um . . . yes, I know," Kelsey said. She felt her tummy tightening with nerves, but still smiled back. She was warming to Jo more and more as time passed, especially after Jo had taken her side about keeping Storm.

"How much does it cost to speak to you now, Your Majesty?" Louise chimed in, doing a silly curtsy.

Anna made sweeping up and down movements with her arms toward Kelsey. "We are not worthy!" she mocked.

Despite herself, Kelsey grinned. "Silence, peasants!" she ordered in a snooty voice, going out of the room, with Storm at her heels.

Jo laughed at the twins' stunned faces. "Good for you, Kelsey!"

Chapter
SIX

Kelsey was just coming out of the bathroom when the phone rang early the following morning.

"I'll get it, Dad!" she called, running downstairs. Storm ran down after her. "Hello?" she spoke into the phone.

"Er . . . Hi. It's me," said a nervous voice.

"Ross?" Kelsey said, looking at Storm.

There was an awkward silence on the other end of the phone. "I . . . um . . . wanted to ask you about this . . . er . . . Wassail thing in the orchard. You must know all about it. You've lived in Long Morton for ages, haven't you?" Ross asked hesitantly.

"Yeah, I was born here," Kelsey said. "Wassail Nights in the old apple orchard are a lot of fun. It's noisy and exciting, and there's yummy food. We always have a great time. But I've never been Apple Princess before. I'm going to be super nervous," she admitted.

"You are?" Ross said, sounding surprised. "I thought it was only me."

"No way!" Kelsey said. "Who wouldn't be worried about having half the town watching them parading about in a cloak and crown?"

"Yeah, I guess so," Ross agreed. "My dad's not very happy about the Wassail ceremony, either. He thinks I'll be making a real fool of myself in front of everybody."

Kelsey suddenly began to realize why Ross might be so quiet all the time.

"Well, for a start, there'll be dancers on Wassail Night, too, and my uncle Billy is one of them. I'd like to hear anyone tell him he looks a fool! He has to duck his head when he walks into our house, and he's about as wide as a wardrobe."

"I'll tell Dad that! He'll be relieved." Ross started laughing.

He had a nice laugh, and Kelsey joined in. "I have to go now," she said apologetically. "I need to take Storm for a quick walk before school."

"You've got a dog?" Ross asked with new interest. "I love dogs."

"Yes. Storm's my new puppy," Kelsey told him. "He's absolutely gorgeous. I usually take him to the park. Hey, you live near there, don't you? We could come get you, if you like."

"Yeah? That would be great!" Ross exclaimed.

"I'll be right there!" Kelsey said goodbye and then hung up. She bent down to bury her face in Storm's soft fur. "I think your magic is working already!"

⁂

Kelsey and Storm passed a neighbor's house on their way to Ross's. Kelsey noticed that there was a new poster in the window. It read, PUPPY WALKERS NEEDED URGENTLY. PLEASE CALL FOR DETAILS. And there was a phone number.

She pointed the poster out to Storm. "I wonder what that's about."

Storm gave a doggy shrug as they walked on.

A few minutes later, Kelsey and Storm

stood on Ross's doorstep as the front door
opened and Ross appeared.

"Hi!" she said brightly. "This is Storm."

Storm woofed a greeting and wagged
his tail eagerly.

"Hello, boy! Aren't you cute?" Ross
said as he bent down to stroke the tiny

puppy. He glanced up at Kelsey. "He's a little King Charles spaniel, isn't he?"

Kelsey was surprised that Ross could tell which breed Storm was. "You seem to know a lot about dogs," she said.

Ross smiled. "I'm always reading dog books and watching shows about them on TV."

"Me too. Dogs are the best," Kelsey said.

As they wandered down the front garden, a stern voice called out, "Ross? Wait there a moment, please."

Kelsey looked around to see a man with shiny, swept-back hair. Ross's dad wore a coat over a smart suit and he was holding a laptop bag. "Hello there, young lady. You must be Kelsey Fisher from Ross's class." Kelsey nodded.

"Hello, Mr. Kirk," she said politely.
"We're taking my puppy, Storm, for a walk
before school."

"So I see." Mr. Kirk eyed Storm, but
he didn't speak to him or bend down to
stroke him as most people did. He looked
at Ross. "Just don't try to talk me into

having a dog. I won't have one of those unruly, messy creatures in the house. You know the rules."

Ross shoved his hands into his pockets. "Worst luck," he mumbled, so that only Kelsey heard him. "See you after work, Dad," he said more loudly.

His dad nodded curtly. "Don't take too long. I don't want you being late for school." He walked past them and down the street.

Kelsey rolled her eyes at Storm. Ross's dad seemed very strict.

"What is 'unruly'?" Storm woofed quizzically.

Kelsey bent down to pat him. "It means badly behaved," she whispered.

Storm drew himself up and his bright blue eyes flashed. "I am not unruly!" he woofed indignantly.

"Of course you're not," Kelsey
soothed. "I think you're just perfect!"

"What are you saying to Storm?" Ross
asked.

"Oh, just stuff about going on walks!"
Kelsey said hastily. "Dogs love that."

Storm barked and danced around,
wagging his tail.

Ross smiled as they crossed the
road and went into the small park. He
produced an empty candy wrapper from
his pocket and scrunched it into a ball for
Storm. Kelsey watched as Ross threw it
and Storm raced about, floppy ears and
swishy tail flying out behind him.

"That's it, boy. Fetch!" Ross cried
happily, throwing the candy wrapper
again.

Kelsey smiled at Ross's face, which was glowing with pleasure; he looked as if he had completely forgotten about being shy.

Chapter
SEVEN

The following day, Kelsey was in class, gluing shiny beads on her crown. Some of the other kids were making drums or putting dried beans into painted tins for musical instruments. She could see Ross concentrating hard as he painted gold squiggles on his crown.

Storm was curled up under Kelsey's desk, watching as she wiped her hands

clean. Kelsey heard him give a little bark
of welcome. She turned to see Jo walking
into the classroom carrying a box and a
big roll of bendy willow.

Jo came over to say hello to Kelsey.
She had come to show Kelsey's class how
to make willow lanterns. "I make woven
willow baskets and garden ornaments for a
hobby," she explained.

"Oh, very nice!" Jo nodded toward Kelsey's crown as she arranged her stuff on a nearby empty desk. "You'll be a wonderful Apple Princess, wearing that."

"Thanks," Kelsey said. She had worked really hard and was proud of how well it had turned out.

"I like Jo," Storm woofed.

"Me too," Kelsey whispered back, surprised at herself. She really meant it.

Making willow lanterns turned out to be a lot of fun. Jo showed everyone how to bend and tie the soaked twigs into shapes. Even Ross seemed to be enjoying himself making an oval-shaped lantern that looked like a spaceship.

"Don't forget to make a little door so you can reach in and light the lantern," Jo instructed.

Kelsey made triangle shapes, which she was going to join up into a star. When one of her willow triangles plopped on to the floor, Storm sprang to his feet in surprise and ran out from under the desk. Growling softly, he bounced down on to his front paws and then grabbed the willow triangle in his mouth and tossed it about.

Luckily, everyone else was too busy to notice. Kelsey had to try really hard not to burst into laughter as Storm went skidding across the room with the triangle, almost falling over his soft front paws.

At the end of the session, Jo gathered up all her equipment. She came to say good-bye to Kelsey. "I could come around early on Saturday. Would you like me to help you get ready? I'm pretty good with sparkly hair spray and silver makeup."

Kelsey nodded. "Yes, please."

"Okay, then. See you later."

Kelsey waved to Jo as she left. She was starting to think that being the Apple Princess might not be so bad after all.

⋆✦⋆

"Oh, yuck!" Kelsey said, as Storm rolled in something particularly smelly in the grass. It was Friday night, and she had decided to take Storm for a quick run in the park on their way home from school.

Storm stood up and shook himself. His whole body rippled and then the movement reached his tail, which twirled about happily.

He looked so pleased with himself that Kelsey burst out laughing. She was

carrying a cardboard box with her finished
crown inside. Placing it on the grass, she
bent down to scratch the tiny puppy
under his chin where the fur was still
clean.

"You messy pup!" she said fondly.
"Pew! You'll have to go straight into the
bath when we get back!"

Kelsey picked up her box again and tucked it under her arm. As she and Storm started walking toward the park gates, Kelsey spotted a familiar figure sitting on a nearby bench. It was Ross.

Kelsey and Storm went over to him. "Hi," she said. "What are you doing here?"

"Oh hi." Ross looked up in surprise. "Just . . . um . . . thinking about tomorrow night. You know, having to lead the Wassail ceremony," he said nervously. "I come here when I want to think about things. It'd be easier if I had any brothers or sisters to talk to, but it's just me and Dad."

"Humph! What's so great about brothers and sisters? My dad's girlfriend has twins. Anna and Louise are always trying to get me to do stuff with them, and they get in my stuff and tease me."

"I wouldn't mind that. It sounds like fun to me," Ross said. "And you'll never be lonely with those two around."

Kelsey blinked at him in surprise. She'd never looked at it like that before.

Ross's face changed. "Are you bringing Storm with you tomorrow night?"

Kelsey nodded. She was planning to make him a little collar later from sparkly wrapping paper. Storm would look very smart as she walked along in her royal robes, holding him in her arms.

"Could . . . could I . . . ?" Ross began.

"What?" Kelsey said.

"I was going to ask you if I could hold Storm for a little while tomorrow night. I wouldn't feel so scared if he was with me. But I'll understand if you say no . . . ,"

Ross said hesitantly.

"Er . . . yeah!" Kelsey said after a second's hesitation. "Of course you can." She swallowed her disappointment. "As long as Storm doesn't mind."

As Kelsey bent down to stroke him, Storm looked up at her with wide blue eyes and nodded. "It is kind of you to put Ross's feelings before your own," he yapped.

"That's settled, then," Kelsey whispered. She stood up again. "You can hold Storm while we're leading the procession."

"Thanks." A wistful smile touched Ross's lips. "You're so lucky. Storm is a really good friend, isn't he? I'm hoping for a puppy for my birthday next week, but Dad's dead set against it."

After Ross had left for home, Kelsey and Storm wandered back through the park. Kelsey's soft heart went out to the lonely boy. "Ross would be great with a puppy, but he hasn't got much chance of ever getting one of his own, has he? Unless . . . Storm! I've just had a brilliant idea!" she exclaimed.

Storm listened intently. When she had finished, he nodded eagerly. "It is a very good plan!"

Kelsey felt a familiar tingling down her spine as Storm's brown-and-white fur glowed with sparks. A shimmery golden mist appeared in the air. In the center of it, a poster formed with writing on it: PUPPY

WALKERS NEEDED URGENTLY. PLEASE CALL FOR DETAILS.

Storm huffed out a stream of golden sparkles. The poster swirled into the air on the cloud of his breath and zoomed away invisibly toward Ross's house.

"I just hope Mr. Kirk gets the message when that plops into the mailbox!" Kelsey said.

Storm nodded. "Me too!"

Chapter
EIGHT

Back home, Kelsey put the cardboard box, with her crown safely inside it, down beside the sofa and then went into her dad's office with Storm trotting along beside her.

"Hello, sweetie. How was school?" her dad said, looking up from his computer.

"Not bad," Kelsey replied. "I was going to make some hot chocolate. Do you want some?"

"No thanks," he said, switching off his computer. "Goodness me, look at the time! I'd better start cooking supper. Jo and the twins will be here soon."

Kelsey found that she didn't mind this unexpected announcement quite as much as she usually would have. Talking to Ross about the twins had made her think a little differently about them. She followed her dad into the kitchen. "What are we having?"

"Spaghetti Bolognese," her dad said, looking in cupboards. "At least, we were," he groaned. "I seem to have run out of canned tomatoes and spaghetti!"

"Da-ad!" Kelsey said, grinning and shaking her head. "Never mind. Me and Storm will run over to the corner store and get some."

"Would you? Thanks, honey," he said,
fishing money out of his pocket. "Then I
can at least make a start."

Kelsey and Storm went to the store.
She paid for the items and as they were
walking, they past a back entry, lined
with a row of garages. One of them was
open, and she heard a fierce snarling and
growling from inside it.

Storm whimpered and crouched

down with his tail between his legs.

Kelsey swept him up into her arms. He was trembling all over, and she could feel his heart pattering against her hands. "What's wrong?" she gasped.

"Shadow must be close. He has used his magic to set those dogs on to me," he whined.

The growling got louder and Kelsey saw two dogs with pale eyes and extra-long teeth peering out of the garage. They'd see Storm at any second!

She started running down the street. There was a bus shelter across the road. It was the old-fashioned kind, with closed sides and an entrance at the front and back. Panting, Kelsey hurtled toward it, dashed inside, and stood there, clutching Storm to her.

Seconds later, she heard the fierce dogs running past. She peered out of the shelter, but they had disappeared around the corner.

Kelsey gave a huge sigh of relief. "It's okay. You're safe now," she soothed. "Those horrible dogs are gone." Now that the danger was over, she felt weak and tired.

Storm gradually stopped trembling, but his eyes were still troubled. "Thank you for saving me, Kelsey. But Shadow will use his magic to make other dogs attack me. If he finds me, I may have to leave quickly without saying good-bye."

Kelsey felt a sharp pang. She wasn't ready to lose her little friend. "Maybe Shadow will go on past and never find you. Then you can stay here with me for good."

Storm twisted around to look up at her, his little face serious. "That cannot happen. One day I must return to lead the Moon-claw pack. Do you understand that, Kelsey?"

Kelsey nodded, but she didn't want to think about it. Maybe if she didn't mention it again, Storm would just stay forever. "Dad's waiting for these groceries. Let's hurry back," she said, changing the subject.

She put Storm down and he scampered along beside her. He seemed to be back to his normal self, despite his nasty scare.

Back in the house, the smell of frying onions greeted Kelsey, making her mouth water. Storm turned his head toward the sound of music and voices from the sitting room. "Someone is here."

"It must be Anna and Louise," Kelsey guessed. She quickly gave her dad the shopping and then went into the sitting room. The twins were practicing a dance routine to their favorite boy-band song.

They looked up and saw her. "Hi, Kelsey. Come and join in!" Anna invited.

"In a minute. I just want to see if Dad needs any help with dinner," Kelsey said.

Louise was doing a complicated twirl. Anna pranced toward her and gave her a playful shove. Louise giggled as she lost her balance and staggered about.

"Watch out for the b—" Kelsey cried, as Louise went to sit down and missed the sofa.

But it was too late. Louise *plonked* down right on top of the cardboard box. There was an ominous crunching sound as it collapsed.

"My crown!" Kelsey gasped.

"Oops!" Louise's hands flew to her mouth as she stood up.

Kelsey opened the squashed box and looked inside in dismay. Her crown was in pieces. "Oh no! Look what you've done!"

"We didn't mean it!" Anna said.

"You never do! You poke into my stuff without asking me, and you're always trying to tell me what to do!" Kelsey fumed. "Why don't you just leave me and Dad alone?" She knew that she was being unfair, but she couldn't help it. Tears sprang to her eyes. She grabbed the box with the ruined crown inside and fled upstairs.

In her bedroom, Kelsey dumped the box on her bed and threw herself down next to it, sobbing angrily.

"Kelsey?" A tiny paw reached out and patted her cheek gently. She turned her head to see Storm peering at her, his little face creased with concern. "I will mend the crown," he offered.

As Kelsey sat up, she felt a familiar

tingling sensation down her spine.
Big golden sparkles ignited in Storm's
brown-and-white fur, and his tail bristled
with magical power. A big fountain of
shimmering gold glitter shot toward the
crumpled box.

Crackle! The box straightened up and jumped to attention. *Bang!* The top flew open and the bits of the crown leaped out on to the floor. *Swish!* The bits jostled about, busily swapping places until they fit together like a jigsaw puzzle. But beads and bits of decoration still littered the bedroom floor.

There was a bright golden flash, which made Kelsey blink hard. When her sight cleared, she saw that the crown was complete. It glistened and glimmered all over like a pair of sparkling fairy wings.

"Wow! It's even better than before! Thanks, Storm." Kelsey gasped delightedly, drying her eyes.

Storm gave her a doggy grin. "You are welcome."

There was a tap on the bedroom door.

"Are you okay?" asked Anna.

"Can we come in?" Louise added.

"Not right now!" Kelsey said hastily. There was no way she could explain how the crown was sitting there in all its glory, miraculously undamaged. "I want to be by myself. I'm going to glue the crown back together, and then I'll come down."

"That's okay. We understand," the twins chorused in a subdued tone.

"We don't mean to boss you around and stuff. We just go overboard sometimes," Anna said.

"I know. And I'm sorry I lost my temper. I didn't mean it about leaving me and Dad alone," Kelsey admitted.

There was silence for a moment and Kelsey thought the twins had tiptoed away.

She heard whispers and then Louise

said, "We wondered if you might like two handmaidens on Wassail Night. We could hold your cloak and stuff, if you like."

Kelsey raised her eyebrows at Storm. She knew that this was the twins' way of saying sorry. "Okay, thanks. That sounds great," she said, grinning.

Chapter
NINE

Saturday morning dawned crisp and clear. "Perfect weather for Wassail Night!" Mr. Fisher announced to Kelsey and Storm over breakfast. Storm looked clean and cuddly and smelled of peach shower gel after the bath Kelsey had given him, although he hadn't been too keen on being bathed at the time.

There was a knock at the front door.

Kelsey's dad opened it to find Jo and the twins. Kelsey's spirits sank when she saw that Louise and Anna were wearing their riding gear.

"Oh no," she groaned softly. Beckoning to Storm, she quickly zoomed into the back garden. "They're going to

invite me to go riding with them again. I just know it!"

Storm looked up from bouncing around in the frosty grass. "Is that a bad thing?"

Kelsey nodded miserably. "Horses scare me, and if the twins find out I'm a scaredy-cat, they'll never stop teasing me about it. I'll just hide out here until they've gone."

"I might be able to use my magic to stop you from being afraid of horses. Do you want me to try?" Storm woofed helpfully.

Kelsey shook her head. "Thanks, but no thanks. I don't actually *want* riding lessons. I'm never going to be crazy about horses like Anna and Louise . . ." She paused as the truth of what she was saying began to sink in. She looked into Storm's calm midnight-blue eyes and she knew what she had to do.

Kelsey went back into the kitchen with Storm in her arms. Jo was sitting at the table and her dad was making coffee and toast.

"I love Saturday mornings at the stables and having riding lessons. Ponies rule!" Anna was saying.

"Are you coming with us this time, Kelsey?" Louise asked.

"Um . . . No thanks," Kelsey said. Her heart was pounding, but cuddling Storm's warm little body gave her courage. She took a deep breath. "Actually, horses make me very nervous. I don't really want to learn how to ride."

Louise looked sharply at her for a

moment and then she shrugged. "Okay."

"No problem," said Anna. "We'll go riding with Mom and then come back here, so we can all get ready for Wassail Night together. It'll be fun."

Kelsey nodded dumbly, too amazed to speak.

"Sounds good to me," Jo agreed. "Let's go, girls."

Kelsey's dad smiled as he poured the coffee.

Kelsey felt a huge wave of relief run through her. She couldn't believe how easy that had been. She glanced down at Storm, whose big blue eyes were twinkling.

It was a clear evening and silver stars
twinkled in the January sky. Kelsey's breath
fogged in the frosty air as she and Storm,
her dad, Jo, and the twins all made their
way to the old apple orchard. Kelsey wore
her shining crown and cloak over her
warm clothes, and Storm trotted proudly
beside her, wearing his smart new collar.

Grown-ups and kids, wearing bright
costumes, were already gathering in
the orchard. Delicious smells of roasted

apples, hot spiced cider and apple juice, and barbecued food filled the air. In one corner, a group of men were keeping watch over a crackling bonfire.

The orchard was a patchwork of gold light and deep shadows. Kelsey saw Ross waiting for her by the old gate with his dad. He wore his crown and cloak. As Kelsey and Storm went over to him, Mr. Kirk smiled warmly at her, looking relaxed in jeans and a sweater.

"You'll never guess what!" Ross said to Kelsey, the moment she reached him. "I'm going to be a puppy walker. It's a really important job. Dad arranged it for me. Isn't that amazing?"

Kelsey beamed at him. "It's fantastic. I'm really happy for you."

Storm wagged his tail.

"Congratulations, Ross!" he barked, which obviously only Kelsey understood.

Ross laughed. "It sounds like Storm's pleased for me, too." He turned back to Kelsey. "Maybe you could help me with the puppy walking sometimes, if you're not too busy with Storm," he said shyly.

"I'd love to," Kelsey said.

"The ceremony's about to start," said Kelsey's dad at her shoulder. "They're calling for the Apple Prince and Princess." Anna and Louise appeared and took hold of Kelsey's cloak.

Kelsey handed Storm over to Ross. Ross's eyes softened as he stroked the tiny puppy's fluffy fur. He gave Storm a cuddle and then squared his shoulders as he handed him back. "Thanks, Kelsey, but it's only right for you to hold him."

Kelsey nodded, smiling. Ross had a
new, confident look on his face. He was
going to be all right. "Here we go," she
whispered to Storm as she and Ross took
their places at the head of the procession.

"This is exciting!" Storm panted
eagerly.

As they moved through the trees
people beat drums, shook rattles and
banged on pots and pans. The gleaming
willow lanterns seemed to float and dance
along. Everyone began singing to wake
the trees from their winter sleep. "Old

Apple Tree, we'll wassail thee . . ."

It was a dramatic moment when everyone stood clear and muskets were fired through the bare branches. *Bang! Bang!* Smoke drifted upward into the cold air.

Afterward, Kelsey was lifted up into a tree to place cider-soaked toast on the branches. Ross had to pour cider down the tree trunk and then their part in the ceremony was over. Then everyone joined in the festivities.

"This is brilliant! It's just like a carnival!" Ross said, munching a burger.

"Told you it was fun!" Kelsey sang out as she went off to get some food to share with Storm. She waved to Anna and Louise, who were taking part in a circle dance.

Just then, Storm gave a whimper of
terror and took off through the trees.

"Storm?" Kelsey noticed sinister, dark
shapes with pale eyes and extra-long teeth
moving through the trees.

Storm was in terrible danger!

Kelsey took off after the tiny puppy,
stripping off her crown and cloak as she
ran. She glimpsed Storm disappearing

behind a wooden hut at the back of the orchard. She ran toward it and had just rounded the building when there was a dazzling flash of bright golden light and a fountain of sparks.

Storm stood there, a tiny puppy no longer but a majestic, young silver-gray wolf with glowing midnight-blue eyes and a thick neck-ruff glittering with a million tiny gold lights. There was an adult wolf with a wise gentle face standing beside him.

Kelsey knew that Storm was going to leave. She didn't want to lose her friend, but she forced herself to be brave. If Ross could be, then so could she.

"Go, Storm! Save yourself!" she said, her voice breaking.

Storm's midnight-blue eyes softened.

"You have been a good friend, Kelsey.
Farewell and be of good heart."

"Good-bye, Storm. I'll never forget
you," Kelsey whispered as tears ran down
her face.

There was a final flash of gold light and a silent explosion of sparks that drifted around Kelsey and sputtered harmlessly to the frosty grass. She heard a frustrated growl behind her as the fierce dogs slunk away.

Kelsey's heart ached, but she was glad that Storm was safe. One day her magic puppy would be the brave leader of the Moon-claw pack. "Take care. Wherever you are," she whispered.

As Kelsey walked back through the trees, she saw Ross coming toward her. His face was glowing with happiness and pride. "Kelsey! I've been looking for you. I can't stop thinking about becoming a puppy walker. It's for dogs that are going to be trained as . . ."

Despite her sadness, Kelsey felt herself

smiling. "Tell me all about it. And don't leave anything out!"

About the
AUTHOR

Sue Bentley's books for children often include animals, fairies, and wildlife. She lives in Northampton, England, and enjoys reading, going to the cinema, relaxing by her garden pond, and watching the birds feeding their babies on the lawn. At school she was always getting told off for daydreaming or staring out of the window—but she now realizes that she was storing up ideas for when she became a writer. She has met and owned many cats and dogs, and each one has brought a special kind of magic to her life.

Don't miss these Magic Ponies books!

Don't miss these Magic Kitten books!

Don't miss these Magic Bunny books!